Forever Love You
Love On

I0556663

J. Love

Copyright © 2016 Jonathan Dekle

www.jonathandekle.com

ISBN: 0692747486
ISBN-13: 978-0692747483

DEDICATION

Here's to those who love.
Who love someone dearly.
Who still are trying to find that dear individual to love.
This is for you all.
May love be forever yours.
Let love be your core.
Let love pour into your very soul.
Let this humble love story tell you to forever love even
more.
For love never dies, it just flows on n' on forever.
—J. Love

CONTENTS

J. Love

DEDICATION

Here's to those who love.
Who love someone dearly.
Who still are trying to find that dear individual to love.
This is for you all.
May love be forever yours.
Let love be your core.
Let love pour into your very soul.
Let this humble love story tell you to forever love even more.
For love never dies, it just flows on n' on forever.
—J. Love

Love On

INTRO

{J. Love}

Here is a story of love, of passion, of seeking after desires to find true love. It's of someone who loves so much that love it self drives him onward to a place only the truest can go. Some may call it a place beyond this world, for few have ever given such a love, but before we get ahead of ourselves, we must understand how a man can seek after love so deeply and passionately until he finds his beloved love.

It all starts back when he is a child. He receives so much love as a child that he think it is normal. Until one day he starts to see the world in a different light. His best friend, being his dog gets shot and when he sees his dog running towards him with blood running everywhere he doesn't know what to do, but to cry. He cries and screams for help! To find there is nothing you can do for his friend. It leaves him so empty inside his heart. It tears a piece of his soul apart from him. He is only nine years old. For days and days he wishes it is just a bad dream. He runs outside to look and look for his friend, to find his best friend truly is died. He cries and cries because his heart is so broken by it. He feels the coldness in the air by it all; emptiness.

As time goes by he slowly gets over it, but never is the same after, at least not for a very long time. He never wants to love ever again as much as he loved his best friend. He can't even love his parents, for he fears the same can happen to them. He starts to feel hate and anger at life. Because he starts to know what lost is. What pain and sadness feels like within. Saddening him for years.

Slowly finding sadness walks with him. He sees just how unperfected the world truly is. For years it drives him to not like the idea of love, because the idea of true love just never seems possible after his beloved dog passed away.

The older he gets, the more he starts to care, for he senses everything. He notices the things people will just simply walk past. The more he starts to connect the realities of things he sees, the world is seen differently by him. As a kid he never knows he does, but as he gots older, he only knew he had to be different. As a kid in middle school he cares so much about the underdog; the person who isn't liked by the rest, because for him, he can best relate to them in the deepest way imaginable.

He comes from a big family, and the love that is in the house is strong, very so, but his older bothers pick on him, which is normal for bothers to do, but for him it is like the whole world coming against him, for his bothers are all he has ever

known, they are his best friends.
All he ever wants is to please
them just so he can be liked, and
loved. He wishes this by everyone,
to see nobody else has the love
he has, so he feels within empty.

Even though his parents love
him to death, his father having
angry problems gives him mix
feelings, and since his bothers
don't seem to love him for him,
he never is able to understand
love from another human in the
way he thinks love should be.

For every time he enacts love,
it hates him for it. He saw the
love of his childhood life get
shot; sees that the only people
who love him is his mom, but he
never allows himself to love her

back fully, for he is afraid of doing so. He loves her deeply, but never can say the words aloud. He knows of love so well, for he sees it so much and even felt it once upon a time that it madden him to the point of hating love. Love breaks his heart over and over and over. How can you blame him for slowly starting to hate love?

By the time he is an early teenager the passions and carvings for the world take him. He falls so deeply into the world he forgets about his family. He starts to fall in love with himself, to the point he thinks he doesn't need anyone else. He views himself as his best friend, and gets consumed by the idea. All he needs is his thoughts to please him, keeping him very content.

By the time he is fourteen, he thinks maybe he will go after a girl, but since his mind and soul is so different it never works out. Because he gives so much of his heart to her that she doesn't know how someone can love like that. He sees her as someone he will marry. He feels that she doesn't love him the way he does her, because she can't match his level of compassion. Perhaps he still doesn't know what love is though, what else make sense?

He doesn't give up rather he instead tries to teach her his love. He sees and learns to find bitterly that she just never was into him as much as he was her. So the love falls apart and she breaks up with him. They both have different pathways to take, so destiny helps break them up, breaking his heart to millions of pieces, that he begins to hate life more and more for what it gave.

He knew he gave all he could, and loved like no other would, but she still wouldn't love him for him. With destiny at work stopping the love to seed, it left him dumbfounded over it all. He starts to wonder after a while maybe he is too different, that love did hate him, but wondered on to why it could be?

His heart is so big, he just knows it, from the compassion he feels. He wonders why he is placed in this world to feel everything, but to receive none of it back in the way he feels. It drives him in raged by this, for he feels peoples emotions better than they feel their own, he swears he does, because he can talk to anyone and talk directly to their soul he feels, but no one else can do that for him. Leaving him crying himself to sleep over it all. For it confusions him.

He feels out of place, so he becomes a loner. Giving up on seeking love; giving up on people in general in a deeper way, for they already have given up on him, he swear it's true.

He becomes self centered, for

self is all he has left. He falls so deeply in love with himself that nobody can make him happy, not even himself after awhile. So he shuts the door of letting anyone in. Every time he would let anyone in they would hurt him, and the pain is almost unbearable. So he locks his heart away letting it to grow cold. He tells himself,

"How can I ever hurt myself?"

He thinks he is playing it safe this way. Over the years he learns what he likes and how people work. He always sees something and reflects it back at himself. Slowly he becomes the odd one in the group. He already is different, but by knowing how people work and what peoples truest desires are, he is able to see through people. Learning to read people as though they say it all to his face.

It becomes a curse, for as he sees everyone being fake, it leaves him to wonder somedays if he isn't just as them, just not admitting it. For he is only a shadow, not a living being interacting with people like the rest. Just on the side lines watching and learning, learning to love the peacefulness in doing just so.

As time goes on he starts to see people as items. For he uses them as items. He is used as one all the time, so he sees it as the way of life. Learning to stop being that way, because as he looks in the mirror he hates knowing he is being 'fake' a 'player'. He wants to be genuine, loving and respectful, so he tries his very hardest to give such a vibe to those he sees deserve it.

He never allows himself to get personally attached to anyone really, and never allows anyone in his mind for too long. He is just too afraid of being hurt again. He develops walls within his heart. Creating so many that he starts to trap himself inside them. Slowly fading away into a deep hole of his own making.

In time he sees life as meaningless. For it truly is to him in the moment. He sees so

much negativity to everything
that the positivity never can
come in to his soul.

For years he is the guy who
sees both sides of the fence. He
will look for the good in
everything before the bad. But as
he pulls himself away from
everyone, he begins to have a self
pity party for himself, to the
point it throws him into a
depression. He begins to see the
negativity before the positive
after a while because he stops
focusing on the positive at all.

Life has always threw him away
as though he was a piece of
trash, so he tells himself. He is a
fighter, he slowly starts to dig his
way back to the surface. As he

climbs higher and higher he sees more and more how much life has to offer. How being positive can truly change your out look to life. How real God can actually be if you let Him be in your daily life, praying daily now, and forever more will.

He starts to feel this sense of loneliness. Him being a loner for years and years is used to this feeling, but now it is a feeling of comfort he is reaching after. A feeling he can't give to himself. He wants a feeling of knowing he means something, but by someone special. A feeling of knowing someone else understands him and loves him for him.

He begins to search for his

love. He searches for years, searching many thousands of miles and as he gets personally attached to girls he sees as someone like himself, he sees that he developed a little of everyone over the years. That he can love a certain part of anyone. Throwing his mind into a wondering spin once this dawns on him. Making him almost having to pretend who he is. For if he shows all he has to offer, who he had become, no one can handle such craziness. Craziness being so much of a person in one person.

Over the years of loner-ship he finds himself more than anyone his age possible ever could, because no one meditated

on self as much as he did and
truly found themselves, at least
he says. Many people 'find
themselves' by others suggesting
who they should be, he allowed
such, but never would enact on
believing what someone else
would say about him unless his
heart and mind would agree with
it also. Till this day he lives so.
Self reflection becomes his daily
process of checking in with
himself you can say. He never
allows anyone to define him,
only God, for God becomes the
only person he can fully trust.

He sponges off everyone over
the years he finds as true,
genuine, honorable, humble, kind,
intelligent, and over all — any
real soul that stands out as

different. The 'regular' people
annoy him, for everyone he sees
who is fake, he feels bad for. He
knows they will never know what
it's like to be a true real human-
being living freely as who they
should be. Even if he knows he
hasn't fully find himself yet
either, he at least is as real as
possible to all he comes across.
He wishes everyone will simply be
themselves — he prays a million
prayers to find those real souls.
He knows they are out there —
they have to be with 7 billion
people living. Leaving him with
little friends until then. It isn't
that he isn't likable, but because
he still is finding his core self.
Still trying to connect his
weirdness with the world,
wondering all along if it will

ever be possible? For rejection
has become his daily song.

He knows the ocean seas are
full with many young women that
are attractive, and even awesome,
but many are in a shallow way, so
he feels, for he never can
connect to them on a level that
keeps him wanting more and in
return they handling all his deep
fast patterned thoughts. He
thinking maybe since he already
is so different, maybe he truly is
meant to walk alone.

Most see him as a crazy kid
who will never say the 'normal'
thing. He says so much they
perhaps never fully follow along
to see he only has a huge
imagination with big ideas, and a

passionate heart, don't judge him for being himself.

He was raised religiously, even though for years he didn't care to talk to God for he thought maybe God truly had cursed him, but he knew it couldn't hurt to pray at least once to find his other half, so he did. Months went on by, and even more months went by. During the months that went by he was happy with life, but he had this deep desiring passion to share life moments with someone else who would understand him for him. Soon years went by leaving him wondering if he truly was lovable?

His living motto is to be the

best he possible can be; being kind to everyone, even if they don't deserve it, he sees it as his purpose to the world to show love, because he understands people better than they will ever understand themselves.

For years he told himself that nobody deserved such behavior from him, but then he realized there will always be more bad people in the world than good, so why be the bad guy when you can be the better person? It only makes sense after a while. His heart and mind agrees to his thinking. God does too, so he feels happy being the good guy now, and chooses too for forever.

By doing this, he hopes to

attract the good souls that are still left, but the old souls, for that is who he is. An old soul trapped in a world of lost and confused souls.

He knows if he wants the girl of his dreams he will have to be the guy of some girls dreams. He thinks it isn't possible, for his past in itself is a nightmare. He was so damaged by it all and so lost in his own head, that how can he ever meet someone who will relate to him? That he begins to loose all hope in finding his forever love.

Chapter 2
{The Meeting}
He is about to give up hope

when one day, at work he runs across this beauty queen. At first in his mind he is like,
"Oh great another beauty, just not for me!",
But he has this feeling inside him to talk to her, so he does.

He smiles and asks if she needs any help? He hears her voice and he thinks it is maybe an angel talking, but catches himself and tells himself not to fall for such again. Since he has a good heart, he still helps her figure out better how the workplace works and guides her along her way.

As she leaves, he has to replay what just happened. As he does, he sees only goodness in the first meeting. So he tells himself if he ever sees her again, he will have to talk to her more.

A day went by, and he doesn't see her, so he starts to let her go out of his mind of thoughts. As he starts to, he sees her. Sees her standing by herself alone. He knows he doesn't have time to talk to her because he is at work and busy, but he leaves wondering just a little bit more on her. Kind of afraid she has already become apart of his mind thinking thoughts without even really even knowing her a bit.

As the day goes on though, just seeing her that one time makes his mind to start thinking things it didn't think about for years. He sees thinking of her as 'passing the time', so there is no harm in doing that, right?

One day he runs across her again, and at first is speechless, he plays it cool and simply asks how her day is going and if she is figuring out the place okay?

As they talk, he can't help but notice how soft spoken and kind she is. That her soul is different than the rest he has meet at work thus far. Some will say that's not possible to tell all that in one moment, but he just sensed it. He knows they must have some connection of some sort. For he always tries to pull the good out of anyone, and some souls have more good to them because they are more compassionate than others, seeing their hearts speak similar languages, he feels okay.

The place they both work at doesn't allow them to talk for long, so since he takes his job seriously he wishes her goodbye, even though he doesn't want to at all.

As he leaves he feels completely horrible. For he never told her his name. The thoughts that entered into his mind made him have to stop and question why such feelings would be running through his heart? He has talk to many girls at work and never felt this way before. They are just like the rest, friendly, but didn't vibe with him, but her, she did vibe with him, he just knows it; he feels it in the air.

The place they both work at is huge, football fields long, it is a warehouse job. Thousands of people work in the mix of them. A few days past and he thinks maybe he will never be able to see her again. The warehouse never allows them to have phones or anything really on them, so he wrote his number down on a piece of paper to give her.

He has had it with him for days, saying, "If I ever see her, i'll have to give her my number." One day he sees her, she is smoking a cigarette and his heart drops, because he told himself he would never go for someone who smokes. He slowly starts to brush the thought of her away, but something deep inside him keeps him thinking towards her. Perhaps destiny working again?

He finally allows the thoughts of her to come back in. He has to battle through it and he finally tells himself nobody is perfect. He looks in the mirror and has a flash back — back to the days he was smoking all the time and drinking and fading away. Back to when he treated his own mom and dad so horrible, and bothers and sisters. He feels so beyond horrible to allow himself to feel like she isn't worth it. For every person is worthy of love.

He thinks if his parents would

of lost hope in him, where would he be today? He tells himself, nobody is perfect and everyone has room for improvement, including himself — we all are continuing to grow and become better versions of ourselves. Aren't we? As he agreed, he felt better.

He goes to work searching so incredibly hard for her, and doesn't see her for hours and hours. He starts to have anxiety attacks over it all, telling him he has already fallen for her, but doesn't want to admit it to himself. Finally after he is about to give all hope up, he spots her. He doesn't care that he is at work, for now he is on a mission. A mission to get his number to her. A mission impossible for there are hundreds of people and many floors she can possible be on.

He has to give her his number, just so he can fully know if she is for him or not. His emotions are rising high, but as he is about to approach her, he tells himself to play it cool. To act like he just hasn't seen her in a couple days, even though he wishes he could tell her it all, but he knows it will be crazy talk to hear a guy say something so emotional. So he accepts the past for what it is and moves forward.

As he is approaching her, he sees her talking to another guy, at first he second guesses if he should still go through with the plan, but he knows if he doesn't it will forever haunt him. So he interrupts and starts talking to her in broad statements basing it off work. He hates making anything awkward, so he tries to play it cool every time, he always over thinks everything, always.

As they walk out of the building, she tells him how thankful she is that he saved her from that guy. He is surprised from hearing this, for it reminded him of himself. For she says, "I was only being kind and polite, I have to do it all the time — it drives me crazy."

When he hears her say that, in his head says check mark. For he does that all the time himself. Not because he doesn't like talking to people, but because sometimes he rather just float in his own mind and not deal with other people at all.

As they walk out and separate, they both smile at each other. As he gets to his car, he jumps to his phone, just to see if she has already texted him. He knows he is in trouble though to have such a mind set already, for it means his heart is already falling for her deeper than he realizes. He knows it is dangerous, but he tells himself it is worth the risk, for so far the risk hasn't harm me, but has helped.

As his mind is spinning over thinking it all, his phone vibrates. At first he doesn't want to even look — for what if it isn't her? He doesn't want to be disappointed, but he has to look, for the waiting so far is already killing him inside. When he sees a number he doesn't recognize, his heart jumps with joy, for he knew it had to be her. Because he never gives his number to girls, ever.

As he opens it, he whispers, thank you God. For no one would message someone that fast if they themselves aren't into someone. As they talk, he begins to notice how different she is from everyone else he has ever ran across. Since he is a loner for years and hardly talks to anyone really, most seem this way to him at first, but he notices that she sees things similar to the way he does, but in a different way. Which makes him even more curious about her. He is nerdy and knows a ton of information about life, but so does she. He thought he had already thought of everything imaginable before, but has to say, "I couldn't possible have."

So he calls her Mystery Women, for she is filled with hidden surprises.

As they talk, time becomes meaningless, which he knows for such a thing to happen he must be enjoying himself, but also that care and passion is going forth. The next day, he sends her a good morning text, and she tells him to eat with her at lunch.

As he parks and is about to put his phone away, he sees her pull right up next to him. Some will say it is just luck, others may say it has no meaning at all, but to him, he sees it as a sign. For out of hundreds of places to park, she parks directly next to him. Like what are the odds of that happening? In a movie perhaps, but real life, what, no way!

He texts her telling her he sees her. She at first thinks it is a joke and even has this face of surprise to her, but then he pushes his horn and she looks up in bafflement. Once she knows who she is looking at, she smiles, and laughs. He laughs and walks her inside.

As they are heading in, she says I forgot something. He is already almost late, so he says he will see her later at lunch, but as he says that, he knows nobody wants to walk alone, so he runs to catch back up with her pretending he also forgot something in his car.

For see, he is trying to hide some of his emotions, because even though he is into her wildly inside his head, outwardly he hides a lot. He still has walls up to protect his heart. The walls are merely small ones, for he knows how much emotion he can express if he is excited and into something, and in this case someone, and the last thing he

wants to do is scare her away
with being overly emotional.

He still isn't sure yet if she is
the one for him. For there hasn't
been enough time spent to know.

Once they get inside he takes
off like a race car to get to his
post. He's sure she must of
laughed some. As the day goes
on, he can't help but think of her,
it is like every bit of him
becomes focus on her. For a
while, he tells himself that is
being overly obsessive, but thinks
why does he feel such a way? Was
that his heart telling him
something?

He isn't sure, for the feelings
he is feeling he can't say he has

ever felt before. He thinks maybe he did once upon a time, but it is strange. His stomach starts to feel those butterflies people talk about, that moment of pure happiness and peace within — he yells at himself to stop feeling such a way, to stop thinking about her if she makes him feel that way. He remembers back to when he is a kid, when he would run with his best friend, his dog, and would feel the freedom in the air by doing so.

Once he went down memory lane with such feelings it drove him with such curiosity. The curiosity being how can someone make him feel that way, and so fast? He knows he has the best walls of protection imaginable for his heart, because for years nobody could knock them down, and within such a short period she could. It scares him at first, but then the more he thinks about it he wonders if that is how true love is? It just happens.

The morning goes by so fast for him, for when he thinks of her time goes away. Lunch comes around, he meets her outside, for she has to smoke. He completely dislikes it, but he doesn't even care, for he is with her. As they eat, he notices how she shares her food with those who don't have as much. This touches his very heart, for it tells him just how nice and caring she truly is. It takes away that scared feeling of thinking about her so much.

The more they talk, the more he begins to fall for her, for there is actually a person who has in-depth meaning to them. Who isn't shallow and naive and stupid. Someone who actually listens and has something to say back. Someone who simply isn't afraid to speak her mind. For him it is like a new being within coming alive. This feeling of power that only love can bring you. It drives his very emotions wild. He still is afraid to show them all though, he wants to take things slow, for he won't dare mess things up.

Lunch goes by so quickly and they have to go back to work. As he goes back to work, he has this since of hope within him, for maybe he surely has found his other half. He runs across her in a hallway and stops and talk for twenty minutes, which is the longest he has stopped working to talk, but he doesn't care, he just wants to know more about her. Work can wait a second.

He walks her to her car after work and wishes her goodbye. He wonders if this is what people feel all the time who are together? He hasn't been with anyone for years, for they never appeal to him in that way. He always asks the question to himself, would I marry her? Every time the answer was no way, no chance at all, but he thought of it then, and the answer was instantly yes. It throws him off, because he doesn't even have to think about it, it just comes to him as though his heart itself spoke for him.

At first it scares him, to think he can fall in love with a stranger, but the more he thinks about it, the more he begins to love it, for he always thought maybe he would be friends for a while and then have such feelings come, but since they came this way he knows only true love can happen like this. The part that scares him the most is how can he hold back such feelings? For he knows maybe she won't feel the same way back, which scares him like crazy.

He goes home, he doesn't even

wait for her to text, but texts her instead. They talk for hours, and he comes to realize just how precious she truly is, and how beautifully perfect she is for him. He invites her over one night and it is the first time they spend time together.

When he first sees her come through the door, it takes his breath away, but he doesn't allow it to show, for he still is afraid she will be too overwhelmed.

As she meets his friends and bothers she says she feels this sense of peace; of welcoming; a feeling she says she hasn't felt in a while. When he hears this it just reassures him even more she is his soulmate. After they talk a while, they drink a little, and are feeling good, then something horrible happens. Something that he wishes never happened.

Chapter 3.
{Mistakes Made}

He has been sober for over nine months and knows he is a better him for being sober. He has a better connection to God and life while being sober, but he caves in because he doesn't see any harm in doing so.

Both of them have stopped smoking weed, for they want to better their lives and be more in control with their emotions. She is thirty plus days sober and him being about nine months sober should of known better.

He knows how weed has messed him up emotionally and how he used to be mentally addicted, and he just doesn't in the moment realize how she is with it. He doesn't fully yet know how much alike they are. In the moment of it all, it is all fun and amazing and it is just for the night, right?

He knows personally with himself, which falls into everyone that you have two sides. A stoner mindset and a sober one. He likes many sides of the stoner side, but knows his sober side is truly the best side of him, for his emotions are in control and with him being so emotional, if his emotions get out of control, it never is good. He can have anxiety attacks and foolishness always follows. He has sound judgment being sober, and he loves that. Clarity tastes good, way better than anything else, he swears.

The night turns out beyond amazing. They talk about their signatures and even practice writing them down. Joking around saying they both one day will have to sign it over and over again, so they mite as well practice now.

They lay in bed and talk for such a long time. He begs her to stay the night, to lay next to him and cuddle, but she can't. She has to head home and says that she'll be alright.

The next morning he is so mad at himself for letting her head home like that, because she couldn't of been sober at all. Thank God she made it home safely.

She would of had work, but

over slept and didn't go in. He invites her for breakfast to a diner. Afterwards they drive two hours away to go hiking. On the way she does her makeup. She is already beyond stunning without any on, but by the time she is done, the words breath taking won't even describe her beauty. For she truly is an angel in his eyes, is flawless.

As they drive they talk about life and have some very deep conversations that are amazing. He begins to see just how much they have in common on all levels emotionally. How her past isn't like his really, but has enough that it is very relatable. Hers has pain and has disappointments in it and it still bothers her. He tries his best to be supportive to give the best advise possible and she does her best to be supportive also. He loves how once she starts talking about something how she will go on and on about it with such passion. For him it truly is an amazing time. Seeing another him, but actually gorgeously beautiful.

Once they get there, both of them being sore from work are invited to smoke again. So they smoke, for they don't see the harm in it. They get stoned, and as they take the hike he isn't as supportive and helpful as he can be, for he is overly stoned. Becomes lost in his thoughts. In the moment of it all it isn't horrible, but as he looks back on it, he hates himself for it. Hates himself so much for it, for he knows he should of been better and should of been stronger and overall there for her.

Knows they should of just stayed home and chilled instead of walking some more as though that very week the both of them didn't walk enough to go again on a walk somewhere else. After the walk they sit down for a little before heading home. He pulls out his phone and shows her an app, a star app. His mind is blown away by the information she already knows about stars, but also for how she wants to learn more. He finds intelligence very attractive.

Soon enough they drive back home, they talk some more on how their day went. Talk about ideas for the future, things to do. Then they both went into their own minds for a little. See he hasn't smoke in such a long time, and neither has she, that when they got high the first few times again, their minds went into a daze, and just weren't in the moment as much as they normally would of been. They both naturally would space off a lot anyways, but this made them space off even more. As they get home he makes some food for work the next day. Then they get into the hot tube and something magical happens.

As they are talking, she comes and lays with him. They both stare into each others eyes. For him, it is as though he in that one moment saw ages of her there right next to him. It is a moment that surpasses all other ones so far, for it is so surreal. They both get out and head to his room. As they are laying there, another almost magical moment happens. They begin to make love, and as they do, the passion and surreality of it is dreamy. Only passionate people can have such a moment. He remembers what time it is, and says he needs to take her home, which kills the mood, and forever changes things so he says. Destiny calling him onward he says.

Instead of just letting the moment happen and letting her know she could of stayed the night. Telling her that the day was beyond amazing since she was apart of it — he for some odd reason kept screwing it up in the smallest littlest ways. It's a day he will never forget, for he feels like maybe if he would of just been more expressive, more open with his emotions she would of stayed. For the meeting and setting was right, but after that night it all turned south. Seeing more and more that with him relapsing like that, how could God bless them? See his past is dark, filled with drugs, alcohol and demons. He made a deal with God to run from such influences, but he didn't fully embrace it. By him doing what he did, he opened his past demons doors open. He knows God forgives him, and will still countless times over, but with drinking, smoking and having sex, it was inviting bad things to happen. He being more stubborn than a trillion mules, he won't give up on her; on love. So he seeks after her still in all the ways he knows how too.

Chapter 4
{Fallout}

As the days go by his heart is already given to her rather she knows it or not. It drives him crazy not knowing how she feels, for he knows something is felt there by both of them. He just knows it. But she doesn't talk to him for days. He knows he had to of made her mad, and sadden her and he feels horrible.

Days later she texts him just

to see what is going on, and he with so many questions tries to play it cool, but can't fully for he loses control of his emotions out of pure worry. Something he isn't aware of until looking back at it weeks later. Which makes him so mad at himself again for being such an idiot with his emotions.

Stressing out he falls back to his past ways, smoking weed and drinking, knowing it only makes things worst in the long run. For he knows he is only half a man living that way.

He still is hopeful she will come back. After about two weeks she does. She doesn't come until late New Years Eve, he promises her he won't be drunk, and

normally wouldn't of been, but he
started drinking just two hours
before she got there. He was
worrying she wouldn't come.
Since he was worried sick about
the whole situation, he didn't eat
anything all day, which didn't
help him with staying sober.

By the time she gets there, he
is already buzzed, it is eight
thirty. He is so incredibly happy
she shows up. She brings with her
wine. It's funny, he doesn't have a
wine opener, so he uses his power
drill to open it. She drinks only
a little. Everybody else by far is
messed up, leaving him just only
hopping she is having a good
time. Since it is New Years Eve,
they all have a fire cracker war.
She is scared completely, leaving

him having to protector her from harm, so they hide behind the hot tube, firing away, he laughing all the way while she is scared to death. Leaving room for him to comfort her and 'save' her.

The best part of the whole entire day was three things: Her coming over, the fire cracker war, and spending time with her alone. The three things he wishes he could fix, and fix again and again are: drinking to much.... Telling her he loved her in that moment, for it wasn't the right time and moment at all and not fully remembering every single precious word she said. It made him wish a million times over it could have a redo button to weeks way back and him never touching any substance at all.

The next morning really early, he wakes to get himself some water and wakes her up to see if she needs any. Completely forgetting how she has trouble sleeping. Wishing he just could just fix those things now, he tries to go back to sleep, but can't, for she is right next to him.

He should of just admired her for a second and fallen back asleep, instead of trying to cuddle with her. Leaving her to not sleep much afterwards. Cuddling could of waited. He feel so horrible for such behavior.

The next morning, her being such a sweetheart, forgives the

whole water awakening and all.
Him still not fully aware of how
she feels, even though she told
him the night before she wanted
to be his girl, he spaces himself,
for he never wants to push, but
after telling her he loves her, he
sees how she only wants to take
it slow. Saw her backing away, he
is afraid. He tries to take it as
slow as possible.

She leaves for a couple days,
not saying much, leaving a
million question to be thought of.
Leaving him loosing complete
hope of her, seeing just maybe
she isn't his other half, just a hair
from being it. Leaving his heart
heavy and sadden for he waited
years for her already, to only
have her ripped away by his own

foolishness. Seeing he doesn't know love yet. That he still has growing himself to do with his emotions, and that he still is only learning what true love is, but aren't we all?

Chapter 5
{Forever Forewell}

A couple of days go by and she invites him to go on a walk with her mom. He gets up very early that day so excited about it. Work and his thoughts were stressing him out, and he knows she will take all that off his mind. She texts him saying her mom doesn't want to go anymore. The idiot he is instead of asking why, jumps and says stupid stuff, stuff he doesn't mean. Him being so inconsiderate, forgetting she is trying to stop smoking cigarettes, just for him, and herself to better herself, just jumps to conclusions. Instead of supporting and being understanding, he does the opposite. Causing her to say screw this guy, and within that moment, looses a lot of hope in what they could of had.

Afterwards he hates himself plentiful, wishes he could fix things. By then she blocks him, and what could of maybe been some incredible love, fades away.

His mind respects her wishes to give her space and leaves her alone. But his heart so thriving, so pushing on to try to fix things, won't listen. Leaving him for weeks on weeks to feel heartache, making him say, "But she worth it all, for I know she is."

He saying again, "But my heart is hers, rather she will take it not, it's hers, for it's open to her."

He says he waited years and years to find her, "I'm done fishing. I will wait and wait until she forgives me. Even if it tares my heart apart, it will stay open to her, for it's hers. For it always has been."

He knew of ways to reach out to her, so he tries, but every time in doing, she blocks him out. He knows he must of hurt her, so he can't ever blame her, ever, for he knows she's only protecting herself. He would of done the same if he was her. How can you blame her, you can't.

Leaving him again reaching out once last time, saying, "I am sorry, sorry for being so stupid, and so emotional unstable, I truly am. Sorry for not valuing all of you. For not thinking of how you may be going through something that I'm not aware of, and I only have made it worst. I am sorry for it all. I am."

He knew words are meaningless to her, that actions is it all, but by him saying this, telling her this, this is him acting out actions the best he knows how too. For words are powerful, meaning he doesn't just say them, he literary means them. Yes sometimes we all say stupid stuff we don't mean, but our actions back it up if it's true or not. Sometimes it's not one or two actions that can tell us the truth. Sometimes it takes many actions to tell if it's true or not.

He tires so very hard to tell her he is sorry. This is the last way he knows how too, by finally accepting it's reality of letting her go, for she has always and only has been a pasting by messenger of love.

Destiny bought them together to teach one another more of love. To help them both grow and become better lovers for the next love they find. To learn lessons of what you want in a relationship and what you don't.

He believes anything is fixable if both parties want to fix things. That if both parties can have deep open communication and be real with one another, they can fall back to the love they found when they first met one another. Sometimes it's better to just let the past be the past, but if you still are in a relationship and it is rough, and it is having it's hard moments, remember God is the glue to love. Invite Him into your life, into your relationship and He can help fix any relationship. It still takes both parties to make things work, but if you both love Jesus and have Him in your lives; I promise your love will grow stronger and stronger — it will grow on forever.

After he gave up on her, not because he wanted to, but because he had too, he realized it wasn't ever meant to be for what was just said. If it was, she would of accepted his apology and would of came home. Leaving him to realize she was only a stepping stone to his true love love. Leaving him so heart felt thankful she was able to help him understand love more and leave him to still love on now stronger and wiser. Now even more loving than before, for now when ever he says SHE, he says it for the she that will come one day, leaving

him to fight to find her still —
puzzling along the way who she
is. Knowing whoever she is, she
must be beyond amazing, beyond
gorgeous from head to toe to
soul, leaving him to forever love
HER, telling ahead of time, baby,
love, darling, I love you
completely, marry me, will you?

One thing you must
understand: He loves all that he
knows of her: meaning there's
surely a lot more to learn. It's
why he simply just wants to be
friends with every girl he finds
matchable. Even if his heart loves
all it knows of them, it will love
all of them, for thats the power
of love, if that makes any sense.
As in, as he meets the hers, he
knows one of them will forever

click and click on both sides leaving the love unbreakable. Leaving the fight for love to grow into a forever flowing fountain of love. For they will love each other so intensely, it will be fire of passion to their very souls.

Here are quotes he has written over time. Love has inspired him to put this together, and he knows she loves little things like this. To be honest, she can jump anywhere in here and find something she'll enjoy. Maybe not all of them she can relate to now, but he promises there will be a lot she will. For he kisses the air hello to her, so she may find him as his forever love, and so he may find also her, his forever love. Hoping by sharing his adventure of love he inspires others with these remaining love words that has touched his very soul. When ever two can connect and begin to love, I pray you will always hold onto love, rather then let it slip away into the thin air. For you can love many, but love only last if two make it last. If two invite God into their relationship, it will last forever. Leaving his love will always be there, but will transfer onto another angel who is even more compatible with him, for he believes God controls it all. Leaving him to never again worry about her or love, rather will let love it self happen when it happens. Telling all that the journey to true real love can be

long and lonesome, but if you stay onwardly loving, love will find you, she will find you, he will find you. #LoveOnForeverU
*)—J. Love

Love Muses

Inspired from seeking love. Designed for single people, for yes the quotes are based off the story, but the overall metaphors can touch us all remarkable deeply. Please,
Forever Love You,
Love Him.
Love Her.
God Bless Love.
Enjoy,
Amen.

{He Chooses Her}
She may ask why he chose her.
He may wonder why she chose him.
He saw her and only saw beauty.
Saw behind that gorgeous face
there also were skeletons of hidden
scares.
Sorrows.
Pains.
But he also saw kindness.
Gentleness.
Caring affection.
Love.
She may see a prince in him, in his
face.
But he knows he wasn't always so.
That he too has hidden skeletons.
Has sorrows, pains, heartaches.
He knows he can enlighten her.
Revive her.
That she can represent him.
That they both can journey on.
In love.
In God.
*)—J. Love

{Falling Together}
It's absolutely incredible how life
works out.
Leaving him knowing God is in
control of it all.
He notices,
She doesn't believe as he,
But he respects what she believes,
Hoping she will respect what he
believes too.
It was in these moments where
things seemed to be falling
completely apart,
That his heart almost dropped to
a million pieces,
Is when it all started to make
sense,
And the flight to a better place
started to slowly happen.
*)—J. Love

{Sought Out Love}

When you're blown away with the
connections made.
When you read through the mouths
and see every connectional
connection connected.
You wish you knew sooner,
But see yourself wasn't even truly
ready.
Even if pain and heartache was
apart of the company,
It was worth it,
For the lessons were needed.
When you find that someone who
is just as crazy;
As heart passionate driven,
Just as complex,
You begin to long to hold them.
For you realize how incomplete
you are without them.
You long to know yourself more,
By knowing them more.
Who knew two souls could take a
journey of discovery as they did.
Who knew love could be as strong

as theirs.
How much faith in God they
could withstand to stand as one in
the end.
In the end it is only the
beginning.
What they created was beyond
what you see in the movies.
For what they created is real,
genuine, and guided on blinded.
But guided on by love,
A love that they both thought
wasn't even possible.
But they fought to prove it is.
They grounded themselves in
love-
To the point it consumed their
very souls.
For they longed for such a love
that it brought them together.
To hold each other forever in love
from above.
*)—J. Love

{Her Being Her}
She has a smart mouth,
But she's as honest as they get.
She's sarcastic,
Mysteries-
But she has a heart of gold.
She's stubborn-
But she's as loyal as they get.
She's a little bipolar,
So sometimes you just gotta laugh
and let her have her way
For you wouldn't want her any
other way.
*)—J. Love

{Thinking of Her}
When you think about her, and
wonder if she is thinks about you
also.
It's a warm feeling moment.
For he knows he loves her
completely.
*)—J. Love
!

*

{The Type}
He's the type who loves even when
none is given back.
The type who sees the bad,
But chooses the good.
The type who doesn't give up on
someone rather fights on for them.
He's the type who loves so much,
That he becomes love crazy.
The type that try's to stay as real
as possible.
For his words and actions is all
he has.
*)--J. Love

{Longing to Talk}
When he wanted to talk to her so
bad,
Just to talk,
but so afraid to because of what
she told him in the past,
All he could do is respect her
wishes and wait for her to want to
talk to him.
It was the hardest thing he ever
had to do.
For his heart told him to talk to
her so badly.
Leaving him sad,
But he respected her wishes so
much,
That it left him heartbroken,
For he loves her so dearly,
That he does it anyways.
*)-J. Love

{Unexplainable Love}
He has a love within him that's so
empowering that his thoughts yet
have found a way to express it all,
Only that the feeling is so real.
When he looks up into the skies,
He sees Gods hand in all of it.
Telling him the love is beyond
heaven sent, hoping she sees it too.
Seeing the devil is bent on ruining
their love.
Praying a prayer to guide the love
on homeward to each other arms.
For loves scent is in the air.
Leaving the unexplainable love
heaven sent without a question.
Whispering into the air,
Love you for you boo.
*)-J. Love

{His Heart}
With such a big heart,
He falls in love with things so
incredible fast,
That when he met her,
She being so beyond
extraordinary,
He couldn't help but fall in love
with her almost instantly.
Because their hearts connected
before they even knew what was
happening.
His heart slowly started talking to
his mind, unwinding his love into
her hearts core.
Pouring love drops each day into
her soul, knowing Angels are
guiding loves hand daily.
*)—J. Love

{Other Half}
When he knew for fact he found
his other half,
He was completely breath taken
away, for she is more than he ever
possible thought she would be.
Just how to break the ice,
To tell her how truly sorry he is
for the past ups and downs,
For not figuring it out sooner.
He always wanted to treat her
right, to be her forever admirer.
To tell her he loves her every
night with a forever kiss.
To not hurt her or put her into a
far off place in anyway,
Only into his arms every night
kissing her goodnight,
Holding her tightly, telling her he
loves her forever.
And always will.
*)—J. Love

{Soulmate}
It's a sad reality:
The more he reaches out,
The more he feels regret,
He begins to wonder if she is
worth reaching out for
Seeking his darling love out.
That he almost stops believing in
what he is trying to do.
Finding his beloved charming
soulmate, his forever companion.
And he knows she is his other side
soulmate.
He knows he is hers also.
She just doesn't believe it yet.
But he just knows it.
Putting his heart into hers,
And putting aside others approval.
For they would never approve
when they can't
see what he sees in her.
Which is pure beauty.
Soul, face to toe.
For she is made of gold,
Covered in diamonds from going

through all hells as he did,
To be made to be so beautifully
adored as his queen,
And he as her king.
Forever.
Whenever he asked himself why he
was still seeking after his love,
he told himself even once he has
her, he will forever be still seeking
after her attention, her respect, her
affection, trying to be her forever
protection, praying above that God
protects his heart, and hers, for he
knows without God, they both
would be nothing great.
So he slams the door of such
negativity, reaching out saying sorry
love for neglecting you, for not
trying to protect our love.
Forgive me, let me take you out
for a star night night and show you
the love I have for you.
*)—J. Love

{Choosing}
When you have two deep thinkers
in love,
That are passionate, caring, and
hesitant,
You have two stubborn people.
Him being a gentle man,
He waits for her to make her mind
up,
For she already knows his has
been made up.
And of course he chooses her over
and over again, forever her.
*)—J. Love

{Soul Talks}
When he put his heart, mind, and
soul into his queen
He is forever saying she will stay
in his being, his heart.
For she touches his very being of
his deepest parts of his heart,
his mind and soul;
Which is a profound moment.
For he realizes he never wants to
live life without her not right next
to his side.
She became his pride and joy.
She brought a spark of life and
light back into his soul.
By her being her,
Which is so simple,
Yet so beautiful for how she does
her is breath taking.
He admires and loves her
completely,
Forever,
For she makes him better, and he
knows he makes her better too.
*)—J. Love

{Love Growing}

Love is a growing process.
When two people come together
and fall in love.
It's them both accepting each other
and saying they want to grow
together,
Want to share their life's together,
And from that they both fall in
love even further,
To the point they are with one
within each other.
And he found that love.
He knows she is that love for him.
For she only makes his love for
her grow more and more.
Just if he can make her love for
herself grow more.
She will understand his love then.
He loves her so much,
That he knows he has enough love
for the both of them.
That he'll wait until one day she
will love again.
For she is his love dove.

His forever love.
If she will believe someone can
love her so much,
She will love herself again.
He will teach her his love forever,
By showing just how much he
loves her.
By pointing out all her highlights
as often as he can.
*)—J. Love

{To Love}
To love someone is to adore them.
Is to accept them where they are
at right now.
Is to tell them the truth,
To listen, share,
Forgive, support,
Build, hold,
Encourage,
Disgust things,
Make stronger,
To bring out the best in each
other,
Give them gifts,
Take out on dates and overall be
their best friend always.
That's love.
That's his love for his queen.
That's the universes love.
God's love.
*)—J. Love

{Her Approval}
All he needs is a sign of yes of
approval,
So he will know she is for real,
That's all,
Then he will move mountains to
get to his love.
*)—J. Love

{End of The Day}
At the end of the day,
Even if he gets busy,
Gets distracted.
His mind will always fall back
unto her,
His love.
Life had a way of taking them
places they didn't think they would
have to go.
But as long as they know how to
get back home,
They will always be with one.
For the love will hold them on
until they are together again.
God, family, love, and fulfilling
life to the best of their abilities will
always be their center focus.
Will always be what their minds
fall back onto to think of.
At the end of the day,
He always prays love will carry
them both on.
That she will join him by his side.
So they will ride life in love.

For Love,
Love from above can set us both
free forever.
Accept my love,
It's yours too have.
You just have to grab hold of me,
And know i'll never let you go.
*)—J. Love

{Loves Whisper}
He whispers love,
Love where are you?
He feeling heartache extra hard
lately.
He can't say it will get better.
But he knows it will.
Wishes he could go to the stars
and back to find what she wants.
Tells her over and over she has
always been enough.
Love, why not love?
Why not let it take over.
Why let something not even
breathe.
How could you know?
When you never allowed it to
move.
To grow—
Stopping it,
Breaking it before it can seed.
Shattering it to pieces.
Leaving him gathering the pieces.
Gluing them back,
Supergluing them back together.

Mending, blending the love back
into her being.
Saying love,
Love is our tick clock talk.
Love is our walk.
Let me mark it,
Mark the love as ours.
You're my forever flower.
My forever admirer.
My forever desire.
I'll climb any tower and sing it
for hours.
It can be ours.
A forever type of love.
Just if you will say yes,
I'll try such a love.
The love will work,
Will connect and work.
For the vibes will collide.
The rise of such an energy will
leave us unstoppable.
Combine God into the equation
and it'll be our life savings.
For nothing Love can even touch
such a love.

Not even the devil.
We be protected by God.
We will love like no other,
For we sought love so long,
So hard,
That once we get the love card,
We will play it in harmony.
That it'll be a forever growing
love that never dies.
He rests his eyes.
Hoping he dies unless she arrives
by his side.
Saying he will never let the love
die.
No matter how many tears he
pours.
He will forever hold on.
Even if he pour tears of sorrow,
Not for himself, but for her.
For the love he offers will forever
be hers to have.
And he can't even imagine her
without it.
*)—J. Love

{A Wish}
He wishes he could read minds,
He is not a mind reader.
For if he was,
He would of found her such a
long time ago.
He can't go a minute without
thinking about her,
At least twice, if not all sixty
seconds.
Multiplied by sixty minutes with
twenty-four hours,
Leaving 86,400 thoughts of her
possible in a day.
Making his day everyday.
He prays at night,
That she will come his way.
So he can spend 86,400 more
moments in a day with her.
So he can spend forever with her
in his arms.
Giving her a forever amount of
rich personal intimacy.
*)-J. Love

{Priceless}
Nothing hurt him more than seeing
his love hurt herself without her
even knowing it.
It makes his soul cry for her.
Making him beg God to take her
burden away so she can breathe
again and know what life is about,
What love is.
So she can be set free and live
again happily in peace, Living loving
life knowing she is beyond loved by
him, by God,
For she is more precious than
gold & silver to him.
Her worth is irreplaceable.
For she is priceless.
*)-J. Love

{Loves Fight}

Sometimes somedays he thinks
walking away has to happen after a
while,
He wonders if letting her go will
change the way he fells towards her,
But knows it won't.
So he leaves the door open as
long as his heart can take.
One day he said he had enough,
He had to let her go,
And started to walk away…..
But then he prayed and God said,
It's your choice, I know you can
take the heartache.
For your heart is golden.
So he stays, for he knows deep
down she is his forever soulmate.
For at the beginning of each day,
Middle & ending,
She always stays in his heart,
Always in his mind.
So he knows he truly loves her,
That he couldn't walk away from
such a love.

For sometimes the closest most
treasured love can come from
waiting just a little bit longer.
For the love is tested and settled
to a full on understanding.
He knows his heart belongs to hers.
For he gave it to her the day they
looked into each others eyes,
Into each other souls,
He knows when they are together,
He is home,
She is home,
They are home.
Home became in each other hearts.
Home became home in each others
arms forever.
*)-J. Love

{Understand Her}
He is always trying his utmost very
hardest to understand her,
So he can know how to be the best
friend possible to her,
Be the best love she will ever
have,
For all he can ever give her is
love,
In anyway possible.
For if she is happy,
He is.
If she is sad,
He is,
For God and her is his all.
His darling
His baby.
His love.
His star.
His boo.
*)-J. Love

{Do Anything}
He'll tell her he's sorry over and
over until she realizes he means it.
He'll tell her over and over he
loves her,
Until she realizes it is true
genuine love.
He'll do anything to prove it is to
her, tell her over and over.
For Love, my heart has always
been yours.
How many more ways do I need
to prove it to you?
*)-J. Love

{Wild Love}
People always tell him he is crazy
for falling in love with a stranger.
He says,
The love is beyond here.
For it is destiny calling them
together.
They just aren't fully ready to
hear it.
He each day is more and more.
He only prays she is too,
For she isn't a stranger to him,
Their hearts speak the same
language.
Leaving them only strangers with
the stories they both have to share.
The connection they have is as
though they known each others
forever.
He knows she only lies about it,
For she is afraid of falling for
him,
For she fell before,
But she didn't just yet understand
him.

His heart,
His love.
Once she does,
He knows she will speak right
back freely.
For she will know whatever she
says, can be trusted by him.
He will only love her for it.
She speaks her heart.
And he admires her completely,
For he knows she will always be
honest to him no matter what,
and he knows he will be to her
too till death does us part.
Saying now and forever,
Love you pretty dorky boo.
Let our love tune play on forever.
*)-J. Love

{Heart Talks}
He knows if she will just let her
heart talk,
Let it speak to her mind,
To drop the walls around her
heart,
It will lead her straight to him,
Even if she thinks it may be a
little crazy right now.
It will guide her to him,
For his love is a magnet.
And she is his negative side,
And he is her positive side.
So once her walls will drop,
He knows the love will connect,
That they will forever connect,
For the love is beyond strong,
That it speaks through the air to
her, whispering, love, love, love
To him it sounds so sweet.
That his love for her,
Will slowly tare down her wall.
For it seeks her so crazily.
*)-J. Love

{The Angel Queen}
Her mind is so completely
beautiful to him,
So completely complex,
Crazy, goofy, dorky, genuine.
For it is beyond fulfilling,
And he only hopes she never will
forget his forever love words.
She is a beauty queen from the
inside out, her soul precious.
His darling angel of love.
Even if he knows she thinks of
herself as the devil.
He sees only the angel.
The queen,
The on growing becoming saint.
For if she will view herself as
some devil,
He knows he must be the devil.
He used to view himself the same
way, hard core bad to the bone.
And that only meant they have the
same minds,
Same hearts,
Same all.

But different,
For she is his other side,
And he knows he is hers.
Just if she will let love in,
She will see what he sees.
The completeness in them both.
Having God guiding them onward.
Homeward, Heavenwards to glory,
To a place only true love lives.
For love is their natural language.
Their love is heaven sent he sees.
He believes, but does she though?
*)-J. Love

{The Wait}
The hardest thing he has to do in
life is wait for her to come home.
The best thing he can do is
uphold patients and love.
To stay busy so his mind won't
think as much about it all.
For then he will have peace
within, Gods peace.
Keeping God first,
Her also in his heart,
Leaving his patients for her
possible no matter what comes.
For if he has already waited years
to find her,
He can wait years more to have
her.
For he will forever love her.
His mirrors reflection of love.
Protecting her as though she is
him, for to him, they are one.
*)-J. Love

{Dreams of Her}
He closed his eyes.
To reopen them within.
To see her eyes.
He visions what she is thinking
about within.
Must be something breath taking.
He looks deeper into her soul
taking him in.
Seeing the most beautiful imagine
to be created.
For he sees her all.
Her kindness attached to the acts.
He sees compartments yet to be
open by their loves journey.
He runs across the one called
forever love.
He can't help but open such a
department.
Looking in to be mesmerized.
He captures it's beauty, and
zooming back out to her eyes.
For now whenever he sees her
eyes, he sees love.
For love has hurt her so bad,

But her being such a fighter holds
onto love.
Fighting knowing the love she
seeks is out there.
That love concours all.
That it tares down walls, to build
new ones as flowers.
That it's power is unstoppable.
He closes his eyes.
To reopen them and she is there.
For he is her forever love.
*)-J. Love

{A Smiles Love}
He always tries to smile.
He always tries to stay positive.
Forever Loving life and her.
He always loves no matter what.
He always stays as patient as
possible, no matter the storm.
And always stays as true and
loyal as he can ever be.
For she is his princess.
His darling.
His baby.
His loving
Queen.
*)—J. Love

{Open His Love}
Sometimes he has trouble
expressing himself to her.
When these moments happen,
He purely loves the challenge,
For it gives him a good puzzle to
figure out for days sometimes,
Even if it drives him silly until he
can fully understand.
He loves solving puzzles,
But loves letting her know how he
always feels towards her.
For to him, hoping her also,
He can tell her anything.
He can give her a free key to
something incredible,
His loving caring heart.
But he can't make her open that
door way,
No matter how incredible the
treasure is inside,
She has to choose to take that leap
of faith to gain such of a gift,
Even if it is offered to her freely.
She still has to choose rather to

open it or not.
He knows one day she will,
So he only loves her like crazy
until she comes home.
For he will always love her like
silly, passionately.
Because she's his baby,
His go to place to talk too.
Hoping she will use him the same
way always and forever.
Having open commutation, hiding
nothing but behind each others
deepest secrets, protecting each
other like their lives depend on it.
He being her knight in amor,
Her being his forever shining
loving queen in beauty.
Placing his arm around her,
telling her every day things will be
okay, no matter what storm comes
their way, he knows God and family
will stay apart of his motto
protecting them forever.
For love is their motto.
*)—J. Love

{Holding On}
Even if it hurts him sometimes,
He knows he won't ever let her go,
He just can't,
For she means way too much to
him, means the world.
That if he is true to himself and
her,
He will never let her go freely,
For he knows deep down he will
never let go of life,
So how can he let go of someone
who adds life to him?
Even if in the moment she isn't
there physically,
She always is in his heart.
In his thoughts.
Rather she knows it or not.
Giving him life in the physical.
He truly cares deeply for his
queen.
So he can never let her go.
For he truly is a genuine soul.
*)—J. Love

{Respecting Wishes}

He can respect her wishes,
Letting her have her own time,
But his heart,
Well that's another story.
For everyday,
All his heart wants is her right
next to his side.
Holding her.
Telling her she'll always be
enough, to stop questioning him.
That she'll always be his.
Standing out above all other
women in the world.
For he cares only about her.
Her soul is beyond gold.
Her body his forever precious.
Leaving every time he looks at
her, he is memorized,
For in his eyes, she is his prize.
*)—J. Love

{Forever Love}
Somedays he feels love doesn't
love him.
That she doesn't want him.
He reaches deep within to hold
onto the love he knows of from up
above, heavens true love.
Somedays he knows she has bad
days too,
Praying for her,
Hoping her bad days soon will go
away forever.
Knowing she needs her space too,
To do her and him to do him.
Somedays he reaches out to get
nothing in return,
Leaving a million questions to
pop up.
Sometimes being foolish believing
the negative thoughts within.
Wanting to run away from love,
Knowing those are his bad days.
Him wanting to go hide under a
pillow and blanket and forget
about everything.

Hoping she will reach out to him
sooner than later.
To reassure him of their love,
That he isn't crazy for loving her
so deeply.
Going back and forth from the
what ifs,
To she is his forever queen,
For the love is heaven sent.
Wondering why he can't just
believe she is his forever love dove.
Wondering if she has the same
questions popping up in her
beautiful head ever?
Seeing love is a game.
Wondering the rules to the love
game?
For to him love has no rules, only
to love forever in every way
imaginable.
Has no games, besides I'll love
you forever you being you.
Building walls up to block out
such negative thoughts.
Protecting the love by reassuring

her and him the love is heaven sent.
That God is present in their love.
Leaving him to know it is a
forever love.
Making him smile, and laughing at
how he can somedays be so bipolar
with his thinking,
Asking God for forgiveness for
ever questioning Him.
Praying He keeps him brave and
strong,
Praying even more that He keeps
his baby stronger.
Asking his baby to forgive him for
ever loosing any hope in her.
Telling her, even if thoughts ever
pop up, at the end of the day,
She is always in his thoughts and
his hearts beating patterns.
For their love is a forever love.
Love you baby.
*)—J. Love

{Heartache Pains}
Him having a heart of gold,
And him feeling as though he is
been rejected sometimes,
Leaves him to wonder why any of
that gold should show somedays?
He is sorry,
He really is,
For he truly is respectable, lovable
and honorable.
But somedays he feels he needs to
release his pain,
For then she will understand he
isn't perfect in anyway,
Only trying to be,
For some days,
He can be a monster with an
angel as his company,
For once he says screw it,
He is just as messed up as any.
Sorrow can turn someone into
someone they are not; it shows their
worst sides, hoping his love sees
past his downfalls. Telling her he
sees pasts her always, only seeing

her forever soul beauty.
Sometimes in those moment we
can be monsters.
He will only have a self pity party
for a second,
And remembers why he hates that
side of him,
For it hides the most precious
part of his being.
His heart; His love.
His gold.
All he ever wants to show is that,
For he lives to show her all he has
which is love,
And if ever he wasn't showing
love,
It never is her fault,
But his,
For it is him viewing life
negatively,
Instead of looking heavenly
And remembering God,
Remembering her,
His angel.
*)—J. Love

{He Must Say}
After a few to many drinks by
your lonesome any can turn into a
nightmare.
He states all of this,
For he never will hide any of
himself from her.
Even if it's someone sometimes
horrible,
He won't hide it,
For he's only human.
Pain and heartache can turn
anyone into someone shameful.
Say you're not like him,
You're lying.
When he wakes,
He'll hate himself.
But he'll state his truest feelings
of hurt for the moment.
So he must ask.
Why will she be so afraid to admit
how she feels?
For he enacts on what he is told.
For to be fully honest,
No one will ever love like he

does.
People will respect it,
But they will never admit it aloud
Like he will, at least not many.
The loving motto he lives.
He calls himself a nightmare,
For lacking the faith somedays to
want to hold onto her,
Onto love.
For he's only frustrated,
With himself,
And only her a little.
For his word is his word.
And his heart his compass.
And his heart points straight to
her every second.
For him to not trust his heart,
Was to give up on himself,
And he hates that feeling.
So he never drinks unless he is
happy,
And chooses to never drink.
For he won't let such thinking
enter his mind,
For he adores his baby to much,

Loves her to much to let a single
word of such inter his mind.
For he knows she is his,
And he is hers forever.
So he must say,
So whenever a bad day happens,
She knows it's him having a bad
day, asking her to forgive him
ahead of time.
Praying she will understand we
all have bad days, even her,
Telling her, he forgives over and
over if ever she takes something out
on him, for he understands life has
it's ups and downs.
Saying let love be what we fall
upon every night.
Going to bed never upset with
one another, only with love in our
hearts.
Sealing it with kisses of
forgiveness.
*)—J. Love

{Future Seen}
As he looks into his future,
He sees her there.
He smiles so big,
For he knows one day she will be
next time him forever.
He pauses to admire such a
thought.
Day dreams on it for miles.
Each time his soul rising higher,
Gaining this power,
Love.
He tells himself,
It doesn't matter how long he'll
have to wait.
He will, because she's his baby.
He will do anything for her.
As he waits,
His love for his princess and
queen only grows.
As he looks into his future,
All he sees next to him is her and
God.
Leaving the rest to be unknown,
For what's the fun in truly

knowing it all.
His trust in God combined with
her into his being,
Set love into the air.
Leaving her to come and find him.
For his love calls every second of
the day for her.
Praying one day soon she'll come
on home to his arms.
Looking into the stars each night,
Wishing a million wishes she'll
come before the next full moon.
Seeing he doesn't need wish's,
He has God guiding.
Wondering how often she thinks
of him, because he thinks of her
often, softly saying,
Baby love you.
Goodnight.
*)—J. Love

{Lonesome Days}
Somedays he wishes he didn't
know how to feel,
For feeling somedays is the most
painful thing imaginable.
For what he feels is her not there,
But feels this love to give her that
is so full.
So plentiful,
That it hurt him,
That he can't share it with her.
He loves life,
But knows,
If she is right next to him,
He will be high off life.
For he will see her and his eyes
will close the door to the negative
forever as their love grows.
He will protector her, help guide
her into brighter days.
Being her shining knight in armor.
*)-J. Love

{Mysterious}
When he knew deep down she has
a secret she is not saying,
Yet so clearly is by what she is
doing by not saying,
It helped reopen his eyes,
He has to wonder why she tries to
stay hidden instead of being open
about it, it's okay to be afraid.
She hiding behind her wall,
When she already is completely
beautiful, head to toe, to soul.
It gives him hope to stay loving.
But loving now even more.
For the door was slowly opening.
Giving him wings to fly to the
skies, to soon she her eyes.
For she's helping to open his eyes,
Praying and hoping only he will
open her eyes also,
That he truly loves her fully,
completely and always.
*)—J. Love

{Eyes Open}
The second he realized just how
truly beautiful she is,
He drops a tear,
For he truly is seeing a reflection
of his own soul.
He always wondered how such a
miracle is possible,
But as he learns more of her,
It all slowly connects.
Sees how wildly expressive and
brave she is with saying what she
feels in her heart.
He adoring loving all he sees,
For he agrees a hundred percent
with her with being genuine.
Sees how much heart she really has
to her loving soul,
Knows how such a heart can snap
and be the meanest all in one.
Sees how she thinks so much she
fights with herself more than she
does the world most days.
Sees how she has been so misused
and hurt, no wonder hearing

someone say I love you, means
absolutely nothing.
For how can it if it has never
been truly meant by someone.
How can she love if love has never
loved her back the way she feels
love should be?
It wouldn't be love then to her in
the way she sees love.
He smiles as he knows she is his
other side.
For he feels the same way.
Knows he also has anxiety,
Thinking maybe she has it more
then he,
Leaving him heartbreaking he
didn't fully understand sooner.
For he knows doubt In self,
Hearing everything negative before
hearing the positive, Knowing how he
can go from racing so high to
falling so low that it leaves him
speechless somedays,
Never knowing why,
Besides allowing to much in all at

once,
So he developed walls that
protected him from the meanness of
the love.
But at the same time it caged him
into a prison den,
So one day he told self to go to
hell— love is better than hate.
"I'm going to go be me,
And let me be free and screw
what anyone says,
As long as I'm doing good,
Knowing my vision and dream,
That is all that matters."
He still to this day having to fight
such feelings somedays,
But he pushes on only trying to
forgive and move on.
Loving all.
Seeing she too feels the same way
on her bad somedays,
Crushing him, because it hurts.
For he always only wants to
support and be there for her.
Repeating a million times over,

And will another trillion times
over times another trillion,
She is a heart warming soul,
A care giving loving human being,
A golden imagine of true beauty,
His forever loving queen,
His soulmate heart connector.
Leaving him to only want her to
speak to him out of love,
For it's hard for him to stay
having such faith all alone.
But he'll hold on forever even if
it almost breaks him,
He will,
For he sees her,
And sees only beauty.
See his type of wild adventure
within her hidden walls.
She likes things he doesn't even
know he will like, he just knows,
And he only knows she will like
things she never thought she would
like either, for their minds connect.
Leaving him to sit back and tell
her relax, it will all be okay.

"We can't over think it.
Just let the past be the past.
Let today be a new day.
Let us just start and never let go.
Will you,
Will you he begs,
Love will you?
Even if you don't today,
One day will you,
For my heart window will always
be open for you to enter in,
My doorway always yours to enter.
For love, dear,
I love you.
Love me,
Love us."
*)—J. Love

{Life's Painting}
As he sees the picture life paints
him, with God directing,
That he slowly is painting,
He only sees lines that point
straight home to a home that never
is a home at all,
But a home in a heart.
His lovers heart.
Leaving him apart,
For his heart isn't near hers.
Leaving him with tears.
But knows one day as the years
go on, she will be by him.
She will be next to his ears,
Whispering love,
I love you.
Love you forevermore.
*)-J. Love

{Always Beautiful}
He'll always fight for her,
For she is golden.
Is precious.
Is breath taking.
He just knows it,
For he believes it.
*)-J. Love

{Loves War}
They say they tired.
He says he sees the signs and
fights for her.
She says,
She sees the signs and waits for
something to happen.
He knowing the love that they
have growing,
Has the devil himself trying to
ruin it, he praying for protection.
He reaches out as far as he is
allowed, saying love, I love you.
While she waits for another sign.
Forgetting the signs are already
being told to her daily.
That the ones she sees sometimes
are only to ruin them.
That she has to make a way to
have him, by reaching out.
For he has already reached his
hands out to the stars,
And all he is doing is waiting for
her to call him from afar to meet
up with him into his arms.

*)-J. Love

{Change the World}
He asks her lets change the world
together forever.
For two is always better than one.
She replies with,
"Yes, let's change it all."
*)-J. Love
!
*

{A Dreamy Dream}
He wishes he can talk to her all
night long,
Talk about the meaning of life.
Talk about how they can only
become better together.
Talk about awesome places to
visit and explore.
Talk about what bothers them,
How they feel, what they want, and
just be so close together they will
never want to leave each other sides
To never want to sleep, for they
always have so much to say to one
another, as their minds spin on.
That to not hear another word left
them both longing to awake to hear
more from each other.
He wishes everyday for her to
come his way.
To say, babe, lets lay all day and
say our hearts out.
Stay by my side,
Touch my thighs,
And lets look at the skies with

wide open eyes and day dream all
day long.
Until we lay,
And kiss every inch of us
goodnight.
*)-J. Love

{His Call For Her}
He can stand as a knight in
armor.
He can be so incredible strong.
He can be so loving,
So patient,
So forgiving and compassionate.
He'll always try his upmost hardest
to stand for what he says.
For he only has his words to give,
She won't allow him to show her
any physical actions.
For she hides herself as the
mystery ghost,
While he shows his affections as a
light to all.
He knows he is strong,
But he is only human,
He can fall somedays,
For his heart longs for her,
It hears her calling,
But never sees her coming.
He sits watching always for her to
come home to him.
Knowing once she does come,

He'll never let her go again.
{Moving Mountains}
Somedays he has such faith,
It'll moves mountains,
Sending signals of light.
While other times,
His mind falls into this pit.
A pit that drains such.
So he calls out to God,
Praying that he won't loose it.
That it'll stay on fire.
Knowing once the faith is tested,
It'll inspire all.
It'll bind them together even more
That with them together:
They truly can be unstoppable.
That no mountain will stop them.
They will create mountains,
Mountains of love.
Exploring loves fountains,
Smiling all a while,
For nature is their second home.
*)-J. Love

{Never Give Up}
He will never give up on his baby.
Never.
He will always fight for her
affection, period.
*)-J. Love
!

*

{Chasing Her}
As he travels he swears he sees her.
Mirror reflections,
Or is it her?
He can't ever get enough of a
look to tell.
But it tells him she is seeking him
in her heart,
But wonders why she does so
secretly.
Wonders why it's at such odd
hours.
For whenever she can't sleep,
Neither can he.
As he travels he sees many,
But only once in a while does he
believe to she her.
Leaving him to say.
Where must he be to meet her, her.
He heads home now.
And will be for the rest of the
day.
For he can't bare to not be there if

she chooses to come home.
For he knows she dreams of him
often.
For at least he does of her all
day long.
Seeing perhaps he never sees her,
Rather wishes he does,
For that's how often she is in his
mind, and how often his heart calls
for her to come home to him.
*)—J. Love

{Purely Love}
As he realizes she doesn't know of
the type of love he has,
His heart drops,
Because everyone deserves such a
love.
He begs to show her his love.
Tells her she already gives him
enough love, by accepting him.
That his heart has enough to pour
out into her, to give her more.
But she never realizes it.
So he tells himself,
He just will have to show her it.
Even if she never will know of it,
He will, because she deserves such,
Plus much more than he can give,
For he knows her heart has just as
much love as he does, but she just
has to embrace it first.
So he shows, as he waits.
*)-J. Love

{Reflection}
As he reflects on things.
He can't help but notice how others
have tried their hardest to block
such a love.
He sees it as the devil trying to
do all in his power to break such a
love.
God isn't to blame,
For it isn't His decisions separating
them.
Rather it's their own.
As in, if there's a will, there's a
way.
It's a string of faith that is
turning from string to chain.
For as the faith grows, the
thickness of the chain does also.
He swears it's so.
For nothing else would make
sense.
For he has been promised all
would be okay.
Just never is told by God the
time it will be.

Only that she will be his,
As long as he stays faithful.
So he does daily.
Hoping she stays seeking him.
Stays true to love,
For love has set both of them free.
For the love is heaven sent.
But do they have enough faith to
believe that?
He does,
He praying so does she.
Knowing she is brave,
Is strong and courageous.
She just has to believe in God,
and in the positivity of life and in
him, that his love is real.
And hers to have.
He kisses the air to her,
Saying, I love you,
Take your time,
And don't stress over anything.
Day by day, breath by breath,
We got this love.
*)-J. Love

{Sorry Love}
To be truly sorry is to understand
why you are.
"So I am sorry,
For not trusting and being the
best I could.
For not being the best example I
could have been.
For not trying to understand you
even better.
For not waiting to be more
patient,
For now I will be.
I'll wait a hundred years over and
over for you.
Sorry for trying so hard to be
apart of something that never yet
was its time to be apart of.
Sorry for trying to figure out the
things that you only could tell of.
Sorry Love,
For not showing all the love that
I truly fully know of.
Sorry for trying to adjust to what
I thought would be acceptable to

you,
Instead of just being me,
Showing all my colors,
Instead of only just a few.
Sorry for not always being the
positive person.
Sorry I am,
For truly what is life without
letting others know they have
messed up, so only then can
correction and understanding
develop, so trust, friendship and
love can be made to stand strong.
Let's improve ourselves until one
day we can look in the mirror and
love every inch of it.
Having God by our side,
Riding life by our selfs,
But happier than ever,
Independent as can be.
Out in the middle of nowhere,
Living just being us.
So then once we meet up,
We won't fully know each other,
But the love we have for life and

God will bring us together stronger
than ever, our hearts talk.
So no matter if we don't know
each other fully yet, it's okay,
We will have ages upon ages to
get to know one of another.
We will have story after story to
tell to one another.
It'll be a time where time won't
matter.
Only that we listen and hear each
other's hearts and voices.
You are my angel,
Shine your light,
And I'll shine mine.
And shall we shine so bright we
will forever be beckons of light to
all we encounter!
For we show love, and live it, for
we know love is the strongest most
power drug there is!
So, sorry love.
Will you forgive me,
And love me for me?"
*)-J. Love

{Crazy How Life Is}
It's crazy how life is.
Growing up,
He never knew he'll move 800
miles from where he was born.
Never knew what place he'll be
when he would fall in love with
someone as her.
They never did either.
Some say it was chance,
He'll say it was God.
She'll say, his crazy.
Who knew where he'll find the
meaning of life, purpose and reason
to breathe another breath.
He never knew, for it wasn't for
him to know.
It was a journey to take, to watch
and experience, to learn, and grow,
mature, and fulfill.
To keep moving forward:
Accompanying with love and
passion.
He'll move on,
Always choosing her,

Growing and moving life's puzzle
pieces each piece at a time,
Smiling, driving life by the ropes.
Praying he'll only be a help to one
another.
Hoping he'll only bring joy and
happiness to all he encounters.
Praying where ever he'll be,
She will want to be also:
For life's always more enjoyable
with someone who see the world
just as you do.
*)-J. Love

{Loved Beyond Words}

She's beloved beyond words.
Purely golden and precious she is.
A devil, that's an angel.
He's a devil trying to be a prince.
Pleading, begging for her to be
the queen he sees so clearly.
Saying they both can learn to walk
again to achieve greatness.
He saying he's just as her.
Purely bad to the bone.
Yet hides it so good.
Saying he's only trying to set an
example, know we can grow.
Saying he has no room to talk.
But he tries to walk such a
gentlemen perfect line.
Smiling saying why won't she?
She says her riches are in who she
is with,
In who she helps, and that money
isn't everything.
But she acts differently.
He saying why can't we walk the
journey together to learn life more.

To be humble enough to ask God
for help.
For all you say you want, He truly
can give.
All the riches in the world, the
devil controls a lot.
But God owns it all.
So if you follow Him, He will bless
you, protect and always be there for
you, for us.
Trust us,
And let the rest fall into place.

Her Eyes to Her Soul
Her eyes prettier than the sun.
Face so perfectly shaped,
That it flashes off everyone she
encounters.
A body, only a goddess could
have.
A soul words can't even express,
besides so precious,
That there isn't another like her.
A mind so complex,
Yet so genius together,

The beauty is breathtaking.
Her misty ghostly self will forever
float on in his mind,
Unless she comes and kisses him.
Then the beauty of her can be
fully opened.
So the love she deserves can be
given to her daily face to face.
So she never will be alone, but
loved beyond measure.
Until then, his book of love shall
be closed.
For it's only for hers to have.
*)-J. Love

{Heart Pitter Pat}
Although he give his all.
In the end was it ever enough?
It isn't his fault.
He tries and gives all he can.
He knows she knows how to reach
him.
Yet she hides and never will.
For he know she still has to
figure out some things on her own.
Leaving him to stop and reflect
back.
Telling himself relax.
Pitter pit pitter pat pat.
Let the heart love back.
Let the mind take control.
Leave the love there.
But control yourself.
And let the thought slowly
disappear;
For it's as simple as saying it's
done.
Filing the thoughts away until she
is ready.
Kneeling down praying,

Dear God!
Forgive me,
For committing treason on love.
I'm weak,
Too weak,
I cant take it any longer.
I'm sorry.
Goodbye boo until a sunny day in
paradise.
Where those eyes shall look and
see centuries of us,
For now they shall be on a self,
gaining dust.
Resting until she is ready.
To open him,
And wants to love again.
When will you love again, love?
When will you be my best friend?
*)-J. Love

{Sky Dreamt Days}
Somedays he looks out into the
sky'
And he sees her;
Smiling.
He tries to wonder where her sweet
soul may be.
But has trouble,
For she's someone still near him
buzzing around like a bee in his
mind.
Roaming searching somewhere for
him.
She's old school,
So she doesn't use her phone.
Leaving him alone wondering why
she just doesn't come home.
Looking up into the sky,
And asking God,
But why?
He lives,
Live free or die hard trying to
give peace to all.
Having to scope out and leave the
rest to God.

As he roams on doing life alone.
He reaches into life to turn its
gears.
Having some fear she never will be
near him whispering,
"I love you dear"
In his ear.
As he lays he grabs his pillow and
whispers,
Love, love, where are you?
I feel you,
But can't touch you.
Sweetie come home why don't you.
Or pick up the phone and whisper,
"I'm coming home."
*)-J. Love

{He Could}

He could fall and never rise.
He could fall and call aloud.
He could love and love forever.
How can he do that?
It's choices.
He chooses to always call aloud
and rise higher.
He'll never give up on love.
For love is on his side.
Love calls him home.
Love lives in his soul.
Love touched his very soul.
Didn't you know?
Has it touched yours darling?
For love is calming.
"Love, will you love?
Why won't you,
Oh why won't you just love.
I'll write a master piece that will
never satisfy.
For the love I have,
Will take a lifetime to give.
To testify.
Love take me home.

Love calls me home.
Even if I am alone,
Love is in my soul.
So I'm always home.
Will you Love come back home?
For I only have half,
You have the other half.
I am broken,
Yet I am yours,
Spoken.
Yet broken.
Until you're back home I'll still be
loving,
But half way broken."
*)-J. Love

{He Calls}
Love he calls.
You there he recalls.
As he falls,
He rests his eyes,
To align with hers in his mind.
He knows she's free.
So he believes she'll be who she
shall be.
He doesn't want her any other way.
She knows the whys to the how's to
the whys he loves her so dearly.
He whispers above clearly.
Love.
Even if I beg myself to not move
away from you,
My heart can't follow.
For it has become apart of my
DNA to say,
I love you.
Stay,
Will you?
*)-J. Love

{Stamped Love}

He says he doesn't care who knows.
Doesn't' care who knows of his
love for her.
It isn't a secret.
It has always been open.
Since his heart was opened.
He pours his love so freely.
Even though he knows others will
judge, he doesn't care.
He tells himself he will be the best
love possible.
Show it in anyway he knows how
to too her, as long as she believes it.
He will turn the impossible to
possible.
Will move mountains with God to
let her know it is true.
Will wait until his heart broke for
her to prove it.
Until she understands his love is
genuine.
Will break all codes of human
love she knows.
For his love is heaven sent.

He will bend the end of time
again and again to prove it.
For his heart is stamped by hers.
Leaving him connected to her
forever and ever.
Leaving her to approve his stamp
of love when she is ready.
For once she will she will be
enlighten with love from above.
Carrying them both home together,
loving each other forever and ever
as God as their guide and leader.
*)—J. Love

{My Angel}
As he thinks of her
He sees her.
Sees why she can't reach out.
He knows she loves him dearly.
Loves so much.
It give him wings to fly.
It makes him cry for the reasons
why.
Why her love is afraid.
He prays he can give her more
faith in God.
For God will protect her.
Save her from such influences.
He begs God day and night to do
so, for he nows God can and will.
And all he is told is give her
time, let her breathe.
He sees her everywhere all the
time, thinking he's love crazy.
Tears come every time he thinks
of her without him by.
For he knows she feels so helpless.
He wishes he can help her.
For she is his.

And he is hers.
For they hold what is called,
True Love.
For their hearts know of the
deepest levels of love.
Leaving why she feels all she feels
all the times,
For to have such a heart as hers,
It is a gift, but a curse all in one,
For she feels everything as he
does somedays.
Leaving him only wanting her by
his side, so he can help,
So he can comfort and care for
her in ways she never know are
possible, besides dreamy.
So she will know just how much
love there is for her to have
whenever she wants it.
That she never has to be afraid,
But understand she is safe.
So she doesn't have to be afraid.
For he helps make her to be brave.
*)—J. Love

{One Day}
One day they both will cry over
wasted time.
They won't forgive each other if
one of them died.
By not being next to each other
sides loving high.
Just if they will drop their pride.
And ride life together forever
being by each other sides.
Things will be better.
"Do you know how precious you
are my darling?
I will move worlds for you.
Collapse mountains,
Create mountains.
Give a forever love fountain.
I'll love,
Forever.
Only
You.
Take my love baby."
Take Gods forever lasting love.
*)—J. Love

{Until We Meet}
He knows one day he will meet
her face to face.
That he wouldn't have to call her,
'her' anymore,
But by her name.
Leaving a whole new love game to
come into the life long loved
picture frame being painted.
For whenever he sees her now,
He only sees lessons in life that he
needs to know to have her.
That when he lays at night and
dreams of her,
He dreams of the love he can give
her so deeply.
Leaving him to know the love he
has is great.
So she will only love him even
greater for him being him.
Leaving that moment itself to
pause and freeze.
Letting the cool fresh air breeze
to remind him God is his first love,
And she will be his third,

Yet will be with one with him,
And he is his second love,
Leaving when they come together,
They will walk as one.
Talk as one.
For they are one.
For she is his one half.
And he is hers.
And God attaches the strings to
hold such a love together,
Leaving in the end, them and
God as their forever love.
Leaving simply one love to live on
and ever, saying,
"Forever Love You
Love On."
*)-J. Love
!
*

Additional Info

Please if you have liked this and been inspired, please Share it.

Also if you ever would like to ask questions: Email J. Love @ j.loveforeveru@gmail.com

Also, for more love relative quotes and topics, follow j.loveforeveru on Instagram.

Again thank you for reading, and may love always live on in you, so it can also live on in others.

*)—J. Love